D0921641

THE TWIN DOGS

CHIHIRO INOUE

Meet the twin dogs.

They don't know who was born first, so they
always argue about which of them is the eldest.

But when they are not arguing, there are lots of things they like to do together!

Taking their parents for a walk.

Drinking milk for breakfast.

Playing catch . . .

. . . and making a mess!

Theirs was a very happy life.
Until one day, when everything changed . . .

The parents brought a new (and very, very loud) creature to the house.

BWAAAA

Suddenly they had to take
strangers out for a walk.

There was no milk
for breakfast.

Worst of all, playing catch
was banned!

The twin dogs were not
happy – not happy at all.

"It's all because of that noisy creature!" they said.

"It's getting all the attention!"

"We want our milk!"

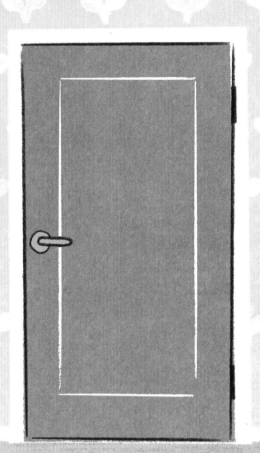

"And we want to take our parents on walks!"

So the twin dogs started to hatch a plan . . .

First, they would sneak out while their parents were resting (they were always so sleepy these days!) . . .

Next, they would create a **HUGE** mess and make them think the creature had done it!

The creature would get into trouble and then everything would return to normal!

They waited and waited until they saw their chance.
"Quick! They've fallen asleep!" they said to each other,
and sneaked into the creature's bedroom.

It was very quiet and they could see
something stirring in the cot.

"Come on. Let's do it!"
they shouted.

And they started to make the **BIGGEST**
mess that they possibly could!

They were very pleased
with themselves!

Now, all that was left
to do was to plant the
evidence.

They climbed up to the cot, and there it was . . .

It was so . . . little!

It actually looked
quite sweet.

But then it opened its tiny
mouth and let out the
LOUDEST noise!

"Shhhhh!" said the twin dogs. "Our parents will know we made the mess if this noise wakes them up!"

They gently tried to calm the creature in the best way they knew.

It seemed to be working. The tiny creature yawned and began to look sleepy. "Phew! That was close!" sighed the twin dogs.

But then the twin dogs also began to yawn, and started to feel very sleepy themselves . . .

In the other room, the parents had woken up.
"Oh, look what time it is!"
"We must have nodded off."

"It's so quiet! Where are the twin dogs?"
they asked each other.

But before the parents could get too cross, they looked into the cot, and what did they find?

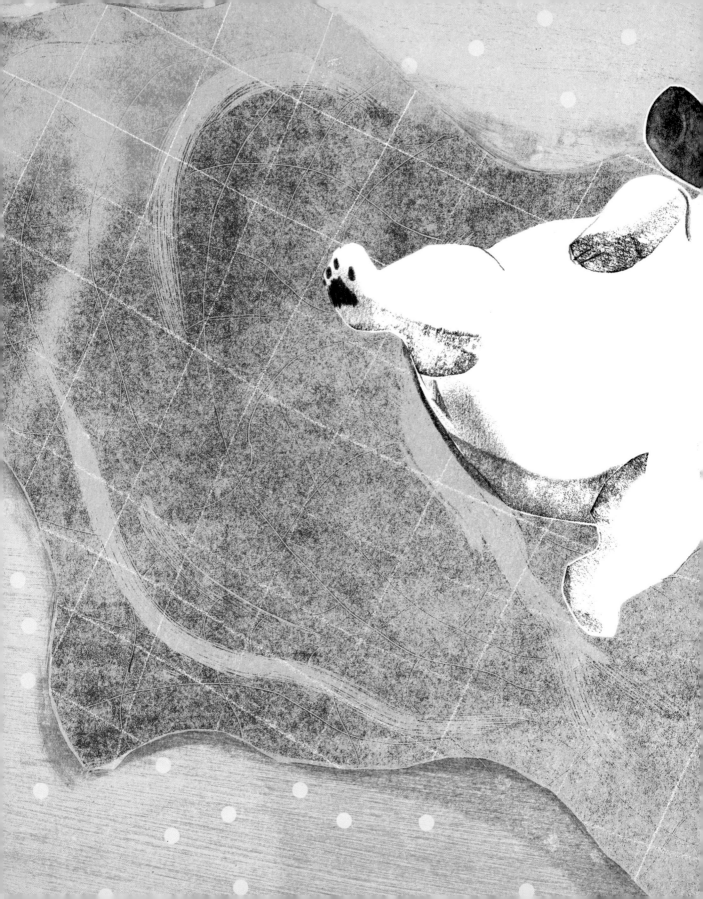

"Oh, look at them, how sweet!"
"See, I told you they would get along!"
"We should have introduced them to
each other earlier, don't you think?"

The parents were so pleased that they forgot to be cross and said "We don't know what happened here, but thank you for taking care of the baby."

"We're sorry if you've been feeling left out.
    You're such good dogs!"

The twin dogs were now very happy to share their parents with the baby.

"We didn't have any reason to be jealous!" they said. "Our parents love us just as much as before. And now we all have more love to share!"

And that is how the twin dogs (who could never agree
which was the eldest) . . .

. . . became the very
best of big brothers.

First published 2020 by order of the Tate Trustees
by Tate Publishing, a division of Tate Enterprises Ltd, Millbank, London SW1P 4RG
www.tate.org.uk/publishing
Text and illustrations © Chihiro Inoue 2020

All rights reserved. No part of this book may be reprinted or utilised in any form
or by any electronic, mechanical or other means, now known or hereafter invented,
including photocopying and recording, or in any information storage or retrieval
system, without permission in writing from the publishers or a licence from the
Copyright Licensing Agency Ltd, www.cla.co.uk

A catalogue record for this book is available from the British Library
ISBN 978 1 84976 722 4

Distributed in the United States and Canada by ABRAMS, New York
Library of Congress Control Number applied for

Colour reproduction by Evergreen Colour Management Ltd
Printed and bound in China by C&C Offset Printing Co., Ltd

To my family and Ken.